PUMPKINHEADS

OTHER BOOKS BY RAINBOW ROWELL

FANGIRL
CARRY ON
ALMOST MIDNIGHT
LANDLINE
ELEANOR & PARK
ATTACHMENTS
WAYWARD SON

PUMPKINHEADS

WRITTEN BY

RAINBOW ROWELL

ILLUSTRATED BY

FAITH ERIN HICKS

COLOUR BY SARAH STERN

MACMILLAN CHILDREN'S BOOKS

First published in the US by First Second,
an imprint of Roaring Brook Press.

This edition published 2019 by Macmillan Children's Books
an imprint of Pan Macmillan
The Smithson, 6 Briset Street, London, EC1M 5NR
Associated companies throughout the world
www.panmacmillan.com

ISBN 978-1-5290-0863-0

3 5 7 9 8 6 4

A CIP catalogue record for this book is available from the British Library.

Designed by Anna Gorovoy
Printed and bound by Bell and Bain Ltd, Glasgow

1

LAST NIGHT
AT THE PATCH

Deja. The Succotash Hut is this way.

I know. I've worked there for three years.

So, where are *you* going?

The Pie Palace.

SUCCOT

PIE PA

What?

Josie, when you look back at your time at the Patch, what's the *one* thing you're going to regret?

Letting Meredith Gomez win MVPPP last September.

You couldn't help that— you had walking *pneumonia!*

I could still *walk.*

Okay, what's the *other* thing you're going to regret?

Oh. *The Fudge Girl.*

In three years, I feel like you could have come up with a better nickname...

She works in the Fudge Shoppe.

I'm well aware.

Tonight is your *last* chance to talk to her.

I *can't* talk to her, Deja. You know I can't.

Josie, you *have* to. You've been mooning over her—loudly and at length—for three years. You can't just *never* talk to her.

I can. I *will*.

That's the plan, actually.

That's *not* the plan.

What are you talking about... Why are you making your unstoppable face?

You and I are working at the Pie Palace tonight. Jaden and Aidan traded shifts with us.

Is that allowed?

It's totally allowed!

But the Pie Palace is—

Right across from the Fudge Shoppe.

Deja... No...

Josiah Templeton, you are a timid little bunny rabbit who has spent three years hiding down in that Succotash Hut from any hope of romance.

I wouldn't say "hiding"—

2
PANIC AT THE PIE PALACE

It was never a campaign. It was a lifestyle.

I love it when you alliterate.

Well, we're not here for any Pie Palace pantry improvement projects.

Presently.

We're *here* to salvage your romantic future.

T minus five minutes, by the way.

FUDGE SHOPPE

I already told you: I'm your *friend*. And friends don't let friends live small lives.

Why are you putting me up to this? You never cared about my "romantic future" before.

I like my small life.

Then why do you complain so much about spending it alone?

I don't *complain*.

I'm...*wistful. Contemplative.* I'm the sort of guy who likes to reminisce about what might have been...

T minus four minutes.

I'm not ready. I don't know what to *say*.

How about— *"Hi, I'm Josiah, I talk a lot about your face."*

That's exactly what I *can't* say.

"Hi, I'm Josiah, I've memorized your schedule."

Deja. Seriously. I need your help.

Okay, okay. Let's role-play this. Pretend I'm Superfudge, and just... start a conversation.

Okay, um...

"Hi, I'm Josiah."

"Hi, I'm the Fudge Shoppy Girl, known to my friends as Marcy."

Marcy...

Maybe don't repeat her name dreamily like she's just handed you the One Ring.

Deja? Did I lose you?

Look at all this pie I've never tried, and tonight is my very last night to do it. I should have planned this better...

FUDGE SHOPPE

3

NEXT STOPPE: FUDGE SHOPPE

I don't have to do this just because you're telling me to.

Everything about our friendship so far says otherwise.

Is...um... is Marcy here?

She's filling in down at the S'mores Pit tonight. The whole Patch is swamped. Can I help you?

Uh, no... Thanks.

GIRLS J
WANNA H
FUDGE

Oh, no...

She rejected you?

She wasn't there to reject me. She's working down at the S'mores Pit tonight.

The S'mores Pit! How does this girl get all the best gigs...

WHUMP

Anyway. Thanks for trying.

Josie. Are you really giving up because of a *change of venue*?

Well, what am I supposed to do? Run down there as soon as the Patch closes?

SHOOM

4
EX MARKS THE SPOT

Do we have time?

This is my last chance to have a double-dipped Granny Smith. We'll make time.

You can always come back to the Patch some weekend as a guest, remember?

Maybe we should stop by the Succotash Hut while we're out, just to check on things.

We really *don't* have time for that—

Hide me. There's my ex.

Which one?

Jess. Don't look.

Which Jess?

Oh, you know...

SIGH

They put that chili fry stand across from us, and now people try to feed the ponies chili fries. It's really unfortunate: Ponies are vegetarians.

SIGH

There's a new chili fry stand?

I stopped by the Succotash Hut earlier to say good-bye, but you weren't there. It was a real scene.

What kind of scene...

36

Right. So...
I'm going
to buy this
caramel apple.

PAPPY'S APPLES

A CARAMEL APPLE A DAY HELPS YOUR DENTIST

Okay...
Good-bye,
Deja. Have a
beautiful life.

Thanks, Jess.
Right back
atcha!

5
STOP, THIEF!

How did you date Jess? She's so...not smart.

She's plenty smart. She's just...more of a pony person than a people person.

DING DING DING

What did she mean, that the Succotash Hut is "a real scene"?

Probably just that it's busy. The whole park is a mob scene tonight.

DING DING

I can't believe that kid stole my caramel apple!

I can't believe you tried to follow him onto the tracks!

I'm going to END that little twerp.

PAT PAT

Yeah you are.

But *first* I'm going to get another caramel apple.

So we both agree that Mission: Fudge Girl is a dead end?

Curse my self-sacrificing nature. Come on.

Thanks for saving my life, I guess.

The train was going pretty slow. I think you would have lived.

6

S'MORE PROBLEMS

You're acting like I'm marching you to your death, not the girl of your dreams. Don't you *want* to meet Vanilla Fudge?

Sort of. I mean, I already like her so much—what's the point of meeting her?

What if our relationship has already peaked?

You don't have a relationship.

You're right. And my favorite part of our non-relationship is the fact that she's never rejected me.

You better make yourself a s'more right away. When she starts laughing at me, I'm going to want to make a quick retreat.

Good thinking, Josie.

P.S. Girls actually *like* it when cute guys ask them out.

Yeah, but I'm not a "cute guy."

I call 'em like I see 'em.

Hey, Dave, how's it going?

It's a nightmare! Did you hear we're oversold? I don't know how they expect us to work like this!

It's not a sword, it's a marshmallow skewer!

KLAK

KLAK

KLAK

Hey, is, um, Marcy down here tonight?

Why? Are you finally going to tell her about your little crush?

I wouldn't call it a *little* crush, Dave.

Well, you're out of luck. She went to get more marshmallows, and they ended up keeping her at the Kettle Corn Kettle. I guess it's a riot up there, too.

Did you hear what happened at the Petting Zoo? Somebody let out Buck!

They let out *Buck*?

54

You seem to be in a bit of a situation.

If you don't put your sticks down, I'll eat all these marshmallows myself!

Looks like you already did!

PLOP

Hey, kid, there's your marshmallow.

AAAAA AAA

7

DEJA VU

So we follow Hot Fudge to the Kettle Corn Kettle—no big deal.

Nah. We're already late getting back to the Pie Palace. Just forget it. This was stupid, anyway.

Don't call my mission stupid!

This is how you always talk yourself out of things, Josie. There's nothing *stupid* about you liking a girl.

Hey. Deja. Do you know where we are?

The S'mores Pit?

This is where we first met! At new employee orientation.

That's right...

I was sitting here by myself, feeling like a big nerd.

And I was like, "Look at that big nerd."

And you sat down next to me.

Remember you tried to teach me a magic trick?

Oh, man. I was so into magic. I used to carry that deck of cards...

I thought it was cool!

You didn't.

Well... I thought it was *funny.*

And you felt so sorry for me that you consented to be my partner.

I didn't feel sorry for you, Josie—I'm not that nice.

Two succotash legends were born that night.

Argh. That's also the first time I saw Fudge Girl. Though she was just "Pretty Pink Headband Girl" then...

Aarrrgh.

Graham-cracker me.

What is it about that girl?

What do you mean?

What keeps so you so... I don't know, *enthralled* after all this time? You've never even talked to her.

I'm not sure. I saw her that night and something *clicked—*

I liked the way she looked. The way she walked. The way she seemed...

Seemed what?

Just the way she *seemed*. Like, it's really easy to imagine good things about her.

I can't decide if that's hopelessly romantic. Or just hopeless.

I always have a better night if I catch a glimpse of her, you know? It makes me feel lucky somehow.

Josiah.

Yeah?

What would happen if we *didn't* go back to the Pie Palace?

Uh...we'd get in trouble?

Probably not.

Why *wouldn't* we go back?

Because we're on a *mission*.

I've decided that you're going to talk to Vanessa Fudgens tonight. And once I've set my mind on something, I won't be dissuaded.

You're suggesting that we just skip...*work*?

We go AWOL.

I can't go AWOL. I'm the MVPPP!

It's just a few hours. And those pie people hardly know us. They'll probably think we're filling in somewhere else.

But they need our help.

Filling in, get it? Pies? Filling?

It seems really irresponsible...

It seems *bold.*

No. I can't skip work.

Hey, guys, wait!

See you never, Dave!

KRUNCH

SMOKESPIT

8

PSL
(PUMPKIN SPICE LIFE)

What?

The smell.

All I'm getting right now is ponies. It's like I'm still dating Jess.

SNFF SNFF

The ponies are part of it. But, also, there's smoke...

There is a *lot* of smoke tonight. What's up with that?

And cotton candy. The cider mulling, the turkey legs roasting—

We still haven't had dinner...

Even the straw and the leaves rotting... The Patch smells like *fall*, you know?

Like every autumn smell all at once.

Next year, at college, fall is going to smell so flat.

Aw, Josie, I'll send you a scented candle.

9
COOL, COOL, COOL

All right, Josie-boy, here's the plan: We're going to march right up to that Kettle Corn Kettle...

...and we are going to *get* ourselves some kettle corn.

Not the bagged kind, either—fresh out of the kettle.

That's the plan?

My mission tonight is to eat as many of my favorite Patch snacks as possible.

I thought your mission was to help me meet Fudge Girl?

It is! But the snacks are a new side mission. We've got the whole night ahead of us now!

I don't see her...

She can't have moved on already. That'd be ridiculous.

THMP THMP THMP

81

Before we leave you to your work, could I just get a small, complimentary sample?

Now beat it.

SCOOP

Hey. Josie.

GOTTA KRAVIN FOR MORE KETTLE CORN? CHECK OUT OUR NEW LOCATION BY THE PUMPKIN DROP!

We came to the wrong Kettle.

Yep. Let's go.

GOTTA KRAUN FOR MORE
KETTLE CORN?
CHECK OUT OUR NEW LOCATION BY
THE PUMPKIN DROP!

Deja, that's on the other side of the park...

We've got nothing but time! It's seven o'clock—the Patch doesn't close for three hours!

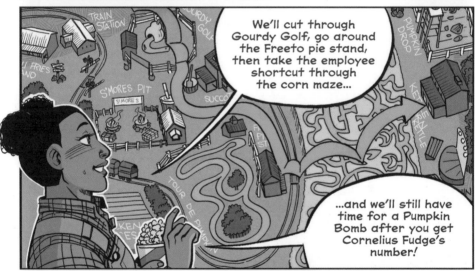

We'll cut through Gourdy Golf, go around the Freeto pie stand, then take the employee shortcut through the corn maze...

...and we'll still have time for a Pumpkin Bomb after you get Cornelius Fudge's number!

What's a Pumpkin Bomb?

JOSIAH! You've never had a Pumpkin Bomb?!

Vanilla ice cream sandwiched between two wedges of pumpkin pie, on a stick, dipped in chocolate...

We have so much to accomplish tonight. Thank goodness we decided not to work!

It's not *that* easy.

It is. I've seen you in action—

"Hi, I'm Deja. I need somebody to follow me around and listen to me be great. You look like a good candidate."

And that's it. They're hooked.

You think I'm great?

Everybody thinks you're great. *And* you have dimples. I'd be a different man if I had dimples.

Well, Josie, if you really think I'm great, think about *this*: In the three seasons I've worked at this pumpkin patch, I've always asked to work with you.

You were *assigned* to work with me.

The first time. After that, it was a choice.

Wait, we can ask for different assignments every season?

Of course we can. Seniority counts.

Then why are we stuck at the Succotash Hut?

Because *you* choose it every year!

I didn't know we could move! *Deja*. We could have been working in the Haunted Hacienda.

Why would you want to work there? People puke in the Poltergeist Tunnel!

Besides, I thought you *loved* the Succotash Hut.

I do, I do. But I feel like I could have made a bigger impact in a higher profile attraction. The pedal cars!

Only football players work the pedal cars. You have to be able to lift the cars if they tip over on someone.

Well, we could have been *someplace* other than the Succotash Hut. We could have been in the *Fudge Shoppe*.

That sounds miserable—three seasons of you working in the very same building as that girl and *still* not talking to her.

You probably would've started dating her.

I don't think Fudge Ripple is into girls.

She hasn't met you yet, has she.

Suffering succotash.

10

SUCCOTASH-TROPHE

What have they done to our succotash?!

How could they mess this up? Actual monkeys could make succotash.

Fine.

But we're not staying!

Deja!

Josiah!

Thank the Lord!

We're not staying. We just came to give you some succotash advice.

Why aren't you stirring, Jaden? You should be stirring!

Like heck you're not staying!

You squirt in some water, and then you stir. It's a dance: Squirt, stir. Squirt, stir.

You squirt and stir. We're getting out of this dump.

You spend your whole life in a Pie Palace, never knowing an honest day's work...

Hey...why aren't *you guys* at the Pie Palace?

Oh, snap.

What do you want to do, Josie?

Stay and make these people some delicious succotash.

Okay, boys, fine. Go back to your Palace. We'll just—

—make a break for it!

What about the succotash?

For God's sake, Josie— true love trumps lima beans!

11

MAKE LIKE
A TREE
AND LEAF

12

TOUR DE PUMPKIN

≷Huff≷

I'm not questioning your decision to run.

But we could have run *in the direction* of the Kettle Corn Kettle.

We've just taken a slight detour.

Which way now?

Around the world.

TOUR De PUMPK

We'll take a shortcut, just past the Pumpkin Tower!

I heard he dragged a fifth-grader through the corn maze.

I heard he ate her ponytail.

I heard Mr. DeKnock put a fifty-dollar bounty on his head—fifty dollars and five free hot-dog coupons.

Wanted. Dead or alive.

I'm pretty sure they want Buck alive—he's just a goat.

Hey, Deja.

Brian, my friend! Can Josie and I cut the line? It's our last night.

Be my guest...

Pedal harder, Josie!

But we're going to miss the shortcut!

Just...a... few more... feet.

Deja, this isn't part of the mission!

This is *vengeance!* Vengeance is an unspoken part of every mission!

But my Fudge Shoppe Girl!

This isn't over!

I hope Jaden and Aidan don't turn us in. Do you think anybody's looking for us? I'm probably going to lose MVPPP over this.

Honestly, I don't think anyone will care.

I *deserve* to lose MVPPP. I'm putting my own needs before the needs of the Patch!

Meredith Gomez is probably delivering a baby in the corn maze right now.

Or teaching thirty Girl Scouts how to make pumpkin butter.

Think of tonight as part of your transition, Josie. You have to move on. You can't stay at the Patch forever.

Todd did. He's been working at the Patch since it opened. Every season! And he's a certified public accountant now.

You don't want to be like Todd! He won't even take his mascot costume off at parties.

The man loves his job.

The man loves wearing a giant pumpkin head. It's like talking to a mime.

Trust me, you don't want to be MVPPP sixteen years in a row.

Think of how many stars there'd be on my nametag...

The world is full of stars, Josie. And also nametags.

117

Relax— we still have *hours* to get to the Kettle Corn Kettle.

13

CHEESY COME, CHEESY GO

Hey there, little kitten, what's wrong?

WAHHHHHH!!!

Do you know where your mom and dad are?

NOOOOOO!

I'll bet we can find them.

The goooastesses came, and I ran away. I'm scared of gooooastesses!!!

WAAAAHHHHHH!!!

Aw, you don't have to worry about ghosts. Ghosts aren't real.

But I saw it! It tried to eat the lady!

But—

Don't argue with her, she knows what she saw.

We're going to help you find your parents. Okay?

WAHHHH

Come on, kiddo, it's going to be all right. Are you hungry?

I've got some candy corn.

I can't take candy from strangers!!!

Oh, right. That's smart.

But I can take... ≶sniff≶

...some Freeto pie.

Really? Are you sure the same rule doesn't apply?

Come on, we'll go back and get you another one. I'm hungry, too.

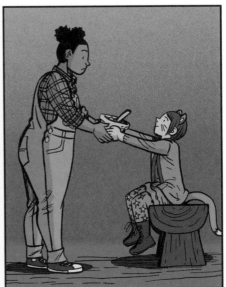

Why doesn't God want me to have snacks?

I'll let you take the bounty for this. Finding a lost kid is primo MV-triple-P fodder.

CORN MAZE

Willa!

MOMMY!

Of course. Thank you...

Deja.

Looks like *I'm* suddenly in the running for MVPPP. I'll thank you both in my acceptance speech.

You don't get to give a speech.

Heyyy, what are you guys doing so far from the Succotash Hut...

Dinner break.

Kind of late for a dinner break...

What are *you* doing so far from the Succotash Hut?

I don't work at the Succotash Hut.

Exactly.

Happy Halloween, Meredith!

14

MAIZED AND CONFUSED

Hey, Deja. Josiah.

Tim!

Tim.

Then maybe I'll see you there.

Y'all be careful in there. You know the employee shortcut?

Left, left, right, right— it's the same every year.

If you get lost, just call me. You still got my number?

Got it.

Well, all right.

He was *this* close to calling you "little lady."

What did you ever see in him?

What's your deal with Tim? He seems like your cup of tea—he's devoted to the Patch. He's worked here since high school.

He's devoted to *himself*. The Patch is just part of his whole...*scheme*.

Scheme?

He's got a scheme! He wants to run this place like a Six Flags!

Tim is the reason we outsource our pumpkin bread.

He said it wasn't appropriate for someone in management to date an hourly employee...

Which will only be a conflict of interest for another seventy-five minutes...

You.

GRAB

NOOOOO!

That little criminal has made a fool of me TWICE.

I'm going to get him banned for life.

How? We don't have a picture of him...

I'll *draw* a picture.

All I wanted to do tonight was help you talk to that dumb girl and get myself some snacks.

Fudge Girl—
M-Marcy—
was shimmering
when we met. That's
why I noticed her.

So you
crush on
her all
year long?

No. I guess not.
It's more of a
Patch thing. Like,
it's one of the
things I get
excited about
every fall...

I didn't think **you** wanted to. I figured you had plenty of winter-spring-summer friends...

I *do.*

Well, I thought I was just your Patch friend.

You *are.*

But we could be outside-of-the-Patch friends, too. We could be friends for all seasons.

You mean we could get together, and, like, *recreationally* make succotash?

If that's what you want, yeah. In the middle of summer.

Deja?

Yeah?

Do you know how to get out of here?

We can just backtrack, right?

Which way did we come from?

Ughhhhhhhh. I'm sorry I got so distracted. How much time do we have left?

It doesn't matter. If we don't make it to the Kettle Corn Kettle in time, then it wasn't meant to be.

This maze doesn't get to decide whether you and Fudge Judy are meant to be. Or whether you talk to her.

You do.

And you're not giving up.

NOD

Boooooooooo ooo ooo

I don't know what you have against fate. Fate brought us together. You and me.

I brought us together. I sat down next to you.

But fate brought us to the Patch...

No, our individual needs and desires brought us to the Patch. *I* needed a job, and *you* love decorative gourds.

No,
I mean—
I can't help it.

While that's
very sweet,
Josie, it isn't
actually true...

You choose to be my
friend every day that
you show up. And I
choose to be yours.

That makes it
sound like work!
I'd rather think
we were meant to
be friends.

But if I felt the same way that you do, we never would have met!

I would have waited for fate to deliver a friend to me instead of sitting down next to you.

Maybe—stick with me here—maybe *that's* why we were meant to be friends.

I was *meant* to meet someone who would take the initiative.

Oh, so you were destined to meet somebody who would do all the work?

Says the girl who lets me make the succotash.

Deja! John Colorado Springs plays their last show down by the Pumpkin Drop!

Which is right next to the Kettle Corn Kettle! We've got to be close!

But, Josie, we're still lost...

SHF SHF SHF

15
LAST CHANCE, JOSIE

Sorry, Josiah. Marcy wanted to catch the last hayrack ride.

She said she'd never been on it, the whole time she's worked here! Isn't that sad?

Yeah.

Sad.

WHEW

Well...thanks, for trying to help me.

What? This isn't over. We know where she is. Go! Now! You can still make it!

Deja, it's pointless! She probably would have rejected me anyway!

You said it *was!*

Probably. But that's not the point! This isn't about true love forever.

It's about reaching for the things you want in life!

It's about being the flipper, not the pinball!

The flipper?

I don't want this girl to achieve *mythical status* in your life just because you never talked to her.

hff hff

hff hff

LEAP

Oh, hey, Todd.

I just need to get by you.

SNORT
SNORT

Is this charades?

SNORT

HRK!

FWUMP

Maybe we could talk later?

16

CARPE HAYRACK!

KATHNK

KATHNK

SNORT
SNORT

KATHNK!
KATHNK!

LUNGE

SNAP!

This is really dangerous and against the rules.

Josiah!

Hi, my name is Josiah.

You know my name.

Your picture's all over the break room.

Oh. Right.

You should sit down. This is a moving vehicle.

Right.

That was really dangerous!

Yeah. Sorry. I don't know what I was thinking. I just really wanted to make the last ride.

Me, too. I've never been on the hayrack before.

What do you think so far?

It's fine.

I guess I'm just bummed because it's my last night at the Patch and—

Me, too. I'm going to miss working here so much!

Oh God, that's not what I meant—I *hate* this place.

You do?

Yes. It's always cold. And dirty—this is basically a dirt-rack ride.

They're the only reason I work here. We're all going to different colleges next year...

We were supposed to ride the hayrack together tonight, on our dinner break—but then I got sent all over the place.

I didn't even get to spend my last night here with the people I really care about.

Josiah! Where are you going?

Back.

Back?

I'm on a mission.

That's extremely dangerous!

And against the rules, I know! I feel bad about it!

17

PUMPKIN BOMB

Todd! Hey! Where do you get Pumpkin Bombs?

OM NOM NOM

Yeah, yeah. Where?

Deja!

hff

Josie... What happened? Did you miss her?

No. And I'm not going to.

I don't understand.

I caught up with her. I talked to her.

To the Fudge Girl?

To Marcy.

No. She's the object of your *confection*.

Get it? *Confection?* Because she works in the Fudge Shoppe.

She *was.* I know. But now I've talked to her, and... I'm not going to miss her. I'm going to miss the pumpkin patch. And I'm going to miss YOU.

I know, Josie—

No. You don't. I'm going to *miss* you, Deja. Like... *really.*

You're my best friend! You're better than my winter-spring-summer friends.

You're better than anyone I know.

Then we can both pretend this never happened?

Okay. Well... What if I *do* like you that way?

I don't know. I've never been in that situation before.

What if I liked you that way a long time ago, then got tired of waiting for you to take the hint?

I'm sorry, Deja. You know how dumb I am.

SNF SNF

SNORT!

What do we do now? I didn't rehearse this.

I think...

We go to Walgreens and buy half-priced candy.

And then we just see.

Deja, you taste like pumpkin.

So, I was just talking to Marta who runs the Cookie Burrow? And she said we could take all of tonight's leftover pumpkin chip cookies...

Also, she told me she's got an in at the department store downtown—she might be able to get us temp jobs next month as Santa's elves.

Santa's elves?! I *love* Santa's elves!

Me, too!

Would we get those shoes? With the little bells?

And all the hot chocolate we can drink! She said a lot of college students work there over break.

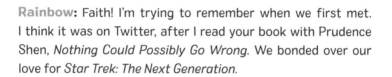

RAINBOW ROWELL AND FAITH ERIN HICKS IN CONVERSATION

Rainbow: Faith! I'm trying to remember when we first met. I think it was on Twitter, after I read your book with Prudence Shen, *Nothing Could Possibly Go Wrong*. We bonded over our love for *Star Trek: The Next Generation*.

Faith: Yes, I remember that! It was pretty soon after San Diego Comic-Con, way back in 2013. I'd been a guest of the show (which was a magical experience) and I'd read your book *Eleanor & Park* on the flight from Halifax, Nova Scotia, to San Diego. I remember literally weeping over this book as I read it, which was actually the second time you'd made me cry. I'd read *Fangirl* earlier in the year and cried over that book, as well. I remember geeking out over your books on Twitter, and someone tweeted my fangirling at you and then eventually we started talking about Star Trek, the great icebreaker. I also remember getting up my courage to send you my graphic novel *Friends with Boys*, which I'd both written and drawn, and you were very kind about it. I really appreciated that.

So that's my memory of how we first met, but I'm trying to remember how you first got the idea to do a graphic novel. I think our publisher, First Second, saw that you were a comics fan and approached you. Is that correct?

Rainbow: ♥ ♥ ♥

You know, I think I connected with First Second on Twitter, too! Yeah, because I was a comics fan. Our editor, Calista Brill, was the person who suggested that you and I work together, and that immediately seemed like a good fit. I could see a lot of resonance between the types of stories that we both like to tell. All your books are very character driven and expressive, and you're especially good at capturing moments, I think. I felt like I could write a story that would feel like both of us.

Though I did initially pitch a totally different story!

Faith: The magic of the internet, haha. Just on a side note: I remember the story you originally pitched, and it was fascinating, but I also remember it had a lot of animals in it. I remember thinking, *Oh no, now I have to learn how to draw all these different animals!*

Pumpkinheads has a few animals (one in particular who plays a prominent role), but not nearly as many as your original story. So I was a bit relieved you changed your mind about what story you wanted to write, as I'm not great at drawing animals!

Rainbow: Ha, that's right. I'd forgotten about the animals! I had a few other story ideas that I played with for a while, too . . . To be honest, I was really sick at the time, and the other scripts I worked on reflected that; they were very heavy and blue, and I felt very heavy when I was working on them. I kept stalling out. Eventually, I decided that I needed to put my brain in a light and joyful place.

I had been hoarding this pumpkin patch setting for a few years. Like, I knew I wanted to do *something* with kids who work at a pumpkin patch. I broke the emergency glass on that idea, and the *Pumpkinheads* script came together so much more fluidly.

Faith: You sent me the script and I read it, and there was a part at the end where I totally teared up. And then drawing that scene was super emotional for me, as well! I don't normally think of myself as the kind of person who gets emotional over comic scripts, so having this reaction, I knew *Pumpkinheads* was special. I immediately sat down and did some rough sketches of Deja and Josiah. I was so eager to get them out of my head and on paper. It's funny looking back at those sketches now because the characters ended up looking so different in the book, but those awkward, early drawings are part of the development process. As characters they just leapt off the page at me. I immediately fell in love with both of them.

Rainbow: I was so relieved that they clicked with you right away. We'd agreed to work together before we had anything locked down—what if this script hadn't connected with you at all? *What if you hated pumpkins, Faith?*

Now that I've worked with a few other comic artists, I've noticed how I write differently depending on the artist, and depending on how well I know the artist. I was glad that I was familiar with your work, because it meant I could write with a lot of trust and confidence. I knew you'd bring so much chemistry to Deja and Josiah's relationship. And I knew that you'd just *nail* the pacing. (Which you did!)

Faith: Thank you! I was delighted with how you chose to write the script because you basically gave me a screenplay with dialogue, action, and emotional beats—but I got to do my own paneling and pacing for the comic. It's personally what I prefer, as I have Strong Opinions on paneling in comics, and how best to draw emotion out of the story. So that was something I really appreciated about collaborating with you on this story. You trusted me to do my thing.

Rainbow: But I did beg you to come to Omaha to visit my favorite pumpkin patch.

Faith: That was a really important trip for me. I don't think I'd have been able to draw the Patch as well as I did without that visit. I got to see the pumpkin patch as a real, lived-in place, full of people and delicious food.

Rainbow: It was very important for you to try Frito pie!

Faith: The Frito pie was very confusing for me at first! I have family in the States, but they're in the south, so I'm not familiar with Nebraska traditions. I was expecting this pie with, like, chips on top of it? And Frito pie is definitely not that. It's cheese and chips and other stuff in this little bag and you eat it with a fork. I remember asking, "When does it turn into pie?" Very confusing for the Canadian!

Rainbow: I think that trip really put us on the same page. We got to walk in Josiah and Deja's footsteps. Also, the script is set in an idealized, fictional pumpkin patch—like the Disneyland of pumpkin patches. So it helped to be in a similar environment and deciding, "Like this!" or "Not like this!" That's also where we had our first conversation about how important color would be in the book.

Thank you for making the trip. I owe you a trip to Canada. ♥

EARLY PUMPKINHEADS SKETCHES

Faith: These are the very first sketches of Deja and Josiah. They look so different here! We decided that they looked much too young in these early sketches, so I went back to the drawing board.

Rainbow: Look at these cuties! My script described Josiah as looking like Paul McCartney, and you can really see Faith trying that here. (I always think of Paul McCartney as having such a kind, gentle face!) Deja was described as "super-cute, like a chubby Gabrielle Union."

Rainbow: The main thing we talked about at this stage was making Josie and Deja look a little older. And I really wanted them to be close to the same height. I wanted to push back on the idea that a girl needs to be small and petite to be completely adorable.

Faith: I think of the character design process as a journey you go on with the characters: In the beginning you're trying to get to know them, who they are, and how best to draw them so their personalities comes through visually. And by time you've drawn the last page in their graphic novel, these characters are your best friends. You know them intimately as people, and that affects how you draw them.

ACKNOWLEDGMENTS

Faith and I would like to thank...

Everyone who helped us bring this book to life (and made the process an unusually joyful one!):

The biggest, shiniest thank-you to my best friend, Danielle Henderson, for inspiring all of Deja's most luminous moments.

And thank you to Leigh Bardugo and Samantha Irby for reading and discussing and actually coming to visit me in Omaha. (I owe you both infinite favors and pumpkin chocolate chip cookies.)

Thank you to Christopher Schelling, who still has *not* come to Omaha, but provided as much encouragement and good advice as he could from Connecticut.

Thank you *like whoa* to Faith's remarkable agent, Bernadette Baker-Baughman; to our editor, Calista Brill, and the crackerjack team at First Second Books; to Sarah Stern, whose colors made this the most *beautiful* pumpkin patch in the world; and especially to the scrupulous Rachel Stark, who came along just when we needed her.

The pumpkin patch in this book is fictional, but Omaha really does have the best pumpkin patches in the world (Faith can attest to this!), and I sincerely hope you get to visit one someday.

Rainbow

MORE SWOONWORTHY NOVELS BY RAINBOW ROWELL

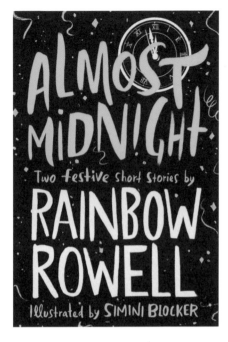

COMING SOON:

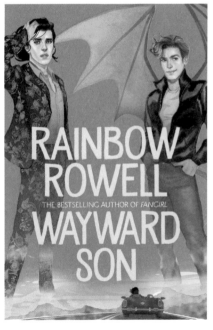